Life Is Forever

Paul Blum

NASEN House, 4/5 Amber Business Village, Amber Close,
Amington, Tamworth, Staffordshire, B77 4RP

Rising Stars UK Ltd.
7 Hatchers Mews, Bermondsey Street, London SE1 3GS
www.risingstars-uk.com

Published 2012

Cover design: Burville-Riley Partnership
Brighton photographs: iStock
Illustrations: Chris King for Illustration Ltd (characters and cover artwork)/
Abigail Daker (map) http://illustratedmaps.info
Text design and typesetting: Geoff Rayner
Publisher: Rebecca Law
Editorial manager: Sasha Morton Creative Project Management

British Library Cataloguing in Publication Data.
A CIP record for this book is available from the British Library.

ISBN: 978-0-85769-606-9

Printed and bound by CPI Group (UK) Ltd, Croydon, CR0 4YY

Contents

Name:
John Logan

Age:
24

Hometown:
Manchester

Occupation:
Author of
supernatural
thrillers

Special skills:
Not yet known

profiles

Name:
Rose Petal

Age:
22

Hometown:
Brighton

Occupation:
Yoga teacher,
nightclub and
shop owner,
vampire hunter

Special skills:
Private investigator
specialising in
supernatural
crime

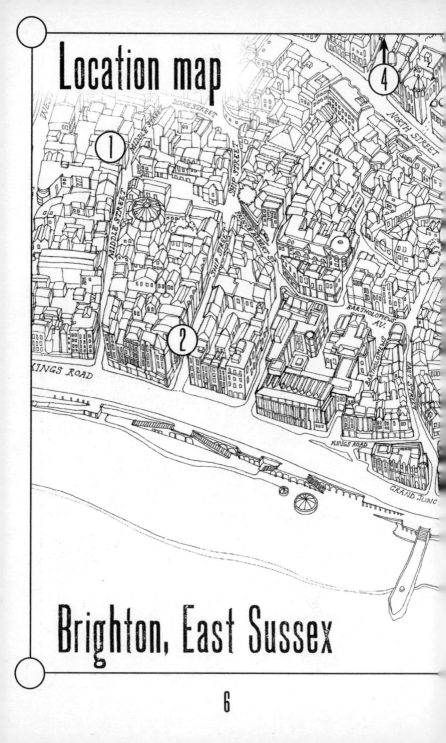

Location map

Brighton, East Sussex

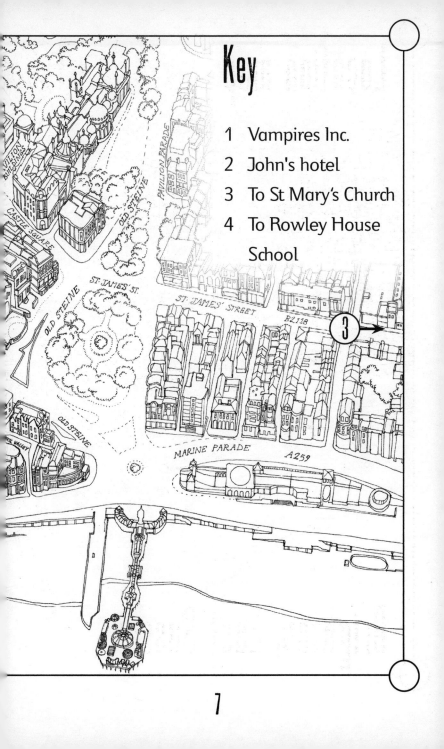

Key

1   Vampires Inc.
2   John's hotel
3   To St Mary's Church
4   To Rowley House
    School

Chapter 1

John Logan looked out of the window of his hotel room and smiled. His room looked out onto the sea, where waves were crashing down on the empty beach.

'No tourists in Brighton today,' he said. 'It's good to get some peace.'

Rose Petal laughed. 'That's how the locals feel every day in the winter,' she said. 'If you're still here then, you'll see what I mean.'

'Maybe by then I won't feel so much like a visitor from Manchester,' he replied. 'Look, I'm even drinking herbal tea! You're training me well.'

Rose Petal blushed. John looked over at her as she sorted out her papers. Rose's hair was bright red and spiky, she had loads of earrings and a tiger tattoo on her shoulder. She was also a great research assistant.

Rose Petal owned a bar and club called Vampires Inc., where Brighton's vampires came to party. She also had a second job as a private investigator. The police even trusted her to help them solve cases involving the supernatural. John was staying in Brighton while he researched his new book about vampires, with Rose's help. Little did he know she would show him a world where vampires really did exist!

'This new case at St Mary's Church is interesting,' she said. 'Harry, the organist, finished his practice there on Thursday evening. He went downstairs to close up, but he heard footsteps behind him. The lights went out in the church and somebody started to play the organ again.'

'That sounds scary,' said John.

'It must have been,' Rose shivered. 'The candles blew out and the church was in darkness. Suddenly, the main lights came on again and the music stopped. The organ loft door swung open but there was nobody there.'

'Weird,' said John. 'But churches do seem really spooky in the dark. What's this got to do with us?'

'Last night one of the women who sings in the choir at St Mary's went missing,' answered Rose.

'Maybe she's visiting family, or gone on holiday,' he said.

'Not likely,' said Rose Petal. 'She works as a singing teacher at Rowley House School. It's still term-time and she lives with her dad. He reported her missing.'

'Is that the school on the hill that looks like a haunted house?' asked John.

Rose Petal nodded.

'So I'm guessing you want to go and talk to the head of the school,' he said.

Rose nodded again. John sighed.

Chapter 2

Mrs Burton was the head teacher of
Rowley House School. As John and
Rose sipped cups of coffee in her office,
she looked out of the window at the
stormy sea and sighed.

'The pupils here are very fond of
Anna Smith. I hope you can find her
soon,' she said, looking at her watch.
'Perhaps I should take you to the
chapel to meet Joseph Judd, our Head
of Music. He and Anna worked very
closely together. He'll just be finishing a
rehearsal with the school choir.'

John, Rose and Mrs Burton hurried
through the grounds of the school. The

wind was still howling and the rain was soaking their clothes. Suddenly, the head teacher stopped and frowned. 'Here's the chapel. Joseph Judd has an office just inside. Good luck, Miss Petal and Mr Logan. Bring Miss Smith back to us safely.'

They shook hands, then Mrs Burton turned and started to almost run back to the main building. John and Rose looked at each other in surprise. The head teacher really hadn't wanted to step inside the chapel. Very odd.

John and Rose opened the door to the chapel. The choir had gone and the only light came from flickering candles. Someone was playing the organ. The old stone building almost seemed to shake as the music pounded around them.

'Okay, this is a bit scary,' whispered John.

Rose Petal nodded and pointed to the back of the church. They climbed the stairs to the organ loft.

'Hello? Mr Judd?' called Rose. The music stopped and Joseph Judd turned from the keyboard. His eyes gleamed red in the dark. Rose took a step backwards and John let out a gasp. He must have imagined it

'Mr Judd? I'm working with Brighton police,' said Rose. 'We wanted to ask you some questions about your singing teacher, Anna Smith.'

'Anna was a great singing teacher,'

said Judd. 'One of the best I've ever worked with.' John peered at him through the darkness of the organ loft. Maybe he had imagined the red eyes, yet Joseph Judd looked odd. He was very pale and it was hard to tell his age from his smooth, white skin.

'Do you know where she might have gone?' Rose continued. 'Or can you tell us anything about her mood on the last day that you saw her?'

Judd stared silently at Rose. John didn't like the way he was looking at her, so he stepped between them.

'What piece of music were you playing just now, Mr Judd?' asked John as politely as he could.

'Bach's Toccata in D minor,' replied

the teacher. He glared at John, who saw his eyes gleam red again. 'It makes me feel alive. It was Anna's favourite too.'

'Did you ever play it at St Mary's Church?' asked Rose.

'No,' said Judd, firmly. 'I spend all my time here. Anna took the choir out to the church, not me.'

But John saw Judd's hands shake as he spoke. He felt certain that the teacher was lying. Without another word, Joseph Judd turned back to the organ and began to play again. The music made a wall of sound and John thought he saw tears in Judd's eyes as he played.

****

They went back to Rose Petal's flat and John turned on his laptop to check his website.

'I didn't like the way he looked at you, Rose. What a creep,' grumbled John.

'Perhaps I remind him of Anna Smith,' said Rose, looking over John's shoulder at the computer screen.

'A man who looks at girls like that shouldn't be working at a girls' school,' said John.

Rose rolled her eyes. 'A man shouldn't, no. A vampire is different. This might be more complicated than you think. Oh, you've got an email through your website. Who's KirstyRHS?'

'Huh? Kirsty what?' frowned John. He read the message out loud.

From: KirstyRHS

To: John Logan, Writer

Subject: Miss Smith

Mr Logan, I saw you earlier when you came to the school. I recognised you from the photo on your book cover. Anna Smith was my singing teacher. There is something that you should know. I wanted to tell you in person, but Mrs Burton didn't want any of us to get involved.

Miss Smith was having a love affair with Mr Judd. Most of the time, she looked really happy about it, but something must have gone wrong. The day before she went missing, she seemed very worried. I could tell she had been crying a lot.

I think Mr Judd is dangerous. I hope you can find Miss Smith soon.

Kirsty

'So, now do you think we should investigate Joseph Judd further?' said John.

'Yes, this is a great breakthrough,' answered Rose. 'I'm going to start some research. In the meantime, reply to Kirsty. Tell her to keep out of Judd's way, just in case.'

That evening, Logan drove back past Rowley House School. The sun was setting over the Sussex Downs and the sea. The sky had cleared, and the views of the rolling green hills and blue water were stunning. 'How could anything dangerous happen somewhere so perfect?' John thought to himself. Whatever evil was going on here, he was determined to stop it.

Chapter 3

The next morning, John was woken up by a loud knocking on his hotel room door. He staggered to his feet, stretching and yawning. As he opened the door, Rose burst into the room.

'Have you seen this?' she cried, waving a newspaper at him.

'As I was sound asleep until about ten seconds ago, that'll be no,' John answered grumpily.

'The body of a pupil from Rowley House School was found this morning. John, it's Kirsty — the girl who tipped us off about Joseph Judd last night. He must have known she suspected him.

He killed her and made it look like she killed herself!' Rose pulled her laptop out of her rucksack and threw it on John's desk in anger.

'Oh no, this is awful. That poor girl,' gasped John.

'There's more, Logan. Joseph Judd is almost certainly a vampire. I did some digging in the old newspaper archives last night. He may have told us the truth that he doesn't play at St Mary's Church now. But one hundred years ago, he was the church organist there.'

Rose pulled up some pictures on her laptop of Joseph Judd dressed in clothes from the 1920s. He looked the same age as he did now. John groaned.

'It's definitely him,' he said. 'But I

thought vampires didn't show up in photographs?'

'They don't. This must have been while he was still human,' sighed Rose.

John was pacing up and down the room. 'So Judd killed Kirsty because she knew he was dating Anna Smith,' he said. 'How are we going to find Anna, if she's still even alive, and make Judd confess to killing Kirsty?'

Rose Petal looked up at John. 'I do have a plan,' she said. 'At nine o'clock tonight, we are going to St Mary's Church to record the ghost that Harry told us about. Anything that plays the organ will be caught on film. It might just give us another lead to help catch Judd before he kills again.'

****

John and Rose got to the church just before nine o'clock. It was pitch-black. The gravestones in the cemetery stuck out of the ground like broken teeth. John shivered. 'It seems I do find churches scary these days.'

'Come on, Logan,' joked Rose. 'You've written a hit book about ghosts and vampires and I'm a supernatural detective. We can do this! Do you want me to go first?'

'Er, yes please,' he whispered, as Rose laughed.

They set up the video camera while Harry finished his practice. At half past nine, Harry turned off the organ and shut the lid. They all went downstairs to the church doors. Just as they got there, the lights went out and the doors slammed shut.

'Here we go again,' said Harry.

John felt his stomach turn over as they heard footsteps echo across the church and climb the stairs. Then the organ burst into life and music bounced off the stone walls.

'Toccata in D minor, by Bach,' said Rose Petal. 'We've heard this piece of music a lot in the last two days.'

'Anna Smith loved it,' said Harry. Suddenly, the candles around the church blew out and the music stopped. Rose and John looked at each other, and ran up the stairs to the organ loft. The organ lid was open but there was nobody there. Rose reached for the playback button on the video camera.

'Look at this,' she said. Logan and Harry looked over her shoulder.

'That's Anna Smith!' said Logan.

'Could that be her ghost?' asked Harry.

Rose shrugged her shoulders. 'I don't know yet. But we can be sure that whatever just played the organ is not a vampire. It wouldn't show up on film.'

Harry gave John and Rose boxes of choir lists and photographs to help them with their research. They took everything back to Vampires Inc. and set to work. It was 3am when Rose Petal looked up and said, 'I've got it. Look at this.' She showed John a photo and a list of names.

'That's Anna Smith,' he said again, rubbing his tired eyes.

'No, it's a girl who looks just like her. Vera Daley was the deputy organist at St Mary's Church nearly one hundred years ago. Maybe she's buried in the graveyard. Let's go and see.'

****

Back at the church, they shone their torches on every gravestone.

'Here it is,' said John. One grave had fresh flowers on it. 'There's a card, too.'

To my darling Vera, I will love you forever. One day, we will be together again.
Joseph

'Is Vera really Anna?' asked John. 'Is Anna a vampire? I'm so confused!'

Rose checked the grave carefully. 'No, I don't think so,' she replied. 'If Vera was a vampire the grave would have been opened. I think the thing we saw on the camera is Vera's ghost.'

'But why would Vera haunt the church?' wondered John out loud.

'And why has the ghost only been seen in the last few weeks, always playing the same piece of music at the same time?' said Rose Petal.

They drove back to Vampires Inc. with even more questions than they had started with.

Chapter 4

Early the next morning, John saw another email on his website. It was from Kirsty! Reading quickly, John gasped and picked up his mobile to call Rose.

reply   reply all   forward

From: KirstyRHS

To: John Logan, Writer

Subject: Meet me

This is Anna Smith. I need to let someone know I'm alive. I heard about Kirsty, and I hacked into her email so I know she contacted you. I'm in London. I'll be at Big Ben at three o'clock. Please meet me there.

Rose and John took the train to London and arrived at Big Ben right on time. They saw Anna Smith walking towards them soon after.

'Thank you for coming, I'm so sorry about all the worry I have caused everyone,' she said. Her eyes filled with tears. 'Kirsty's death is my fault. She saw Joseph and I together once, but I made her promise not to say anything. She was my best pupil. I knew she would try to find me, then I saw the news report about her death. I shouldn't have run away ...' Anna broke off and sobbed.

Rose put her arm around Anna's shaking shoulders. 'You must have had good reason to leave,' she prompted.

'I loved Joseph so much,' she sobbed. 'You won't believe the truth about him, though.'

'He's a vampire,' stated John. Anna gasped as John continued. 'Rose is a private investigator. She works on vampire cases all the time.'

'I didn't believe vampires were real. I only found out how wrong I was last week,' said Anna. 'Joseph was so relaxed about it. I never felt scared with him for a moment. But then we had a big row. Joseph said he loved me so much that he wanted me to live with him forever. He wanted to turn me into a vampire, too.'

Anna wiped her eyes and carried on speaking. 'Joseph's first love was a girl called Vera. He showed me an old photo of her. She could have been my twin sister. Joseph loved her very much, but her father would not let them marry. One night he went to the church and killed his own daughter!'

'Did he kill her while she was playing Bach on the organ? At nine o'clock?' asked Rose carefully.

'That's right,' said Anna. 'The sheet music was lying by her body.'

'Vera's ghost has returned to haunt the church,' Rose explained. 'She must have been troubled that you and Joseph were getting so close.'

'Who knows?' sighed Anna. 'I just knew I did not want to be a vampire. I don't want to live forever. Joseph got

so upset and angry when I told him,
I thought he might try to change me
anyway. That's why I ran away.'

Big Ben struck four o'clock. John,
Rose and Anna looked at all the people
around them. For them, life was not
forever but they were luckier than
Joseph Judd for it.

Chapter 5

John and Rose Petal found Joseph
Judd in the school chapel just as the sun
was starting to set. He was staring at an
old photograph of Vera and didn't look
at them as they entered the room.

'Anna won't be coming back, Joseph,'
said Rose. 'You need to let her go. And
you need to confess to killing Kirsty. It's
all over.'

To their dismay, Judd began to cry. 'I
want to die. I am so sick of this life, of
being alone. I just want to fade away
and be with Vera.'

'Rose knows other vampires who can
help you,' John said softly. 'Come with us.'

But Judd just let out a shout of pain and leapt to his feet. He pushed Rose out of his way and shoved John to one side. He was a blur as he ran up the steps to the organ loft. Within seconds, they heard a thud, followed by a high-pitched shriek.

'Joseph!' yelled Rose. She led the way back outside and, in the last rays of the sun, black ash fluttered down on them from above.

'He killed himself,' gasped John. 'He burnt to death in the sunlight ...'

'... rather than face life alone,' finished Rose. 'Even vampires get lonely, John. They need someone, too.'

Together John and Rose walked back through the gardens to the school.

They would keep Joseph Judd's secret. Anna Smith was safe. But neither Rose nor John would ever forget what they had seen. Love, it seemed, was forever after all.

Glossary

Bach – a famous German music composer

breakthrough – a piece of information that adds new and important knowledge to solving a case

cemetery – a place where dead people are buried, also known as a graveyard

complicated – difficult

organ loft – the place in a church where the organ stands

pounded – sounded very loud

private investigator – a person who investigates crimes instead of the police and is paid to do it

Sussex Downs – an area of open land in the south of England where people can take walks and visit nature reserves

Quiz

1 Who owns the bar called Vampires Inc.?

2 What animal is tattooed on Rose's shoulder?

3 What is the name of the singing teacher at Rowley House School who has disappeared?

4 What colour eyes does Joseph Judd have?

5 What new information does the email from Kirsty to John Logan reveal about the missing woman?

6 Where do Rose and John go to make a video recording of the ghost?

7 What piece of music does Joseph Judd play on the organ?

8 Who murdered Vera?

9 Why did Anna run away to London?

10 Why did Joseph Judd kill himself?

Quiz answers

1 Rose Petal

2 A tiger

3 Anna Smith

4 Red

5 Anna and Joseph were having a love affair

6 St Mary's Church

7 Bach Toccata in D minor

8 Her father

9 She did not want Joseph to make her into a vampire

10 He did not like the thought of living forever on his own

About the author

The author of these books teaches in a London school. At the weekend, his research takes him to the beaches and back streets of Brighton in search of werewolves and vampires.

He writes about what he has found.

The Vampires Inc. books are available now
at your local bookshop or from
www.risingstars-uk.com

RISING ★ STARS

Freephone 0800 091 1602 for more information